Where's Father Christmas?

Find Father Christmas and his festive helpers in 15 fun-filled puzzles

Written by Danielle James
Illustrated by Harry Bloom
Design by Graeme Andrew

JB
JOHN BLAKE

Published by John Blake Publishing Ltd,
3 Bramber Court, 2 Bramber Road,
London W14 9PB, England

www.johnblakepublishing.co.uk

First published in hardback in 2013

ISBN: 978 1 78219 476 7

British Library Cataloguing-in-Publication Data:

A catalogue record for this book is available from the British Library.

Design by www.envydesign.co.uk
Printed and bound in the UK by Butler Tanner & Dennis Ltd, Frome, Somerset

1 3 5 7 9 10 8 6 4 2

Papers used by John Blake Publishing are natural, recyclable products made from wood grown in sustainable forests. The manufacturing processes conform to the environmental regulations of the country of origin.

Father Christmas's Mission

Merry Christmas friends!

Do you want to hear a joke? Oh good, I love jokes! *What do elves learn in school?* Have you got it yet? *It's the Elf-abet, of course*!

My name is Jingle, by the way, and I'm Father Christmas's number one elf. I live in Lapland with Father Christmas, but I sleep in the elf barn with all my friends. We help Father Christmas sort the sacks of letters that flood Lapland in December, make toys, organise presents and load everything onto the sleigh. Because I am Father Christmas's number one elf, on Christmas Eve I'm allowed onboard his sleigh to help him deliver the gifts! We don't just work hard on Christmas Eve, though. All year round we are busy keeping an eye on everybody to check they are behaving. Last year, because there were so many good girls and boys, we were really busy making more toys than ever before. It was snow joke.

This year, because everyone worked so hard, Father Christmas has said that some of my friends can join us and, as a special treat, we can play some games on our journey around the world. I've asked Bells the snowman and Eugene the penguin to fly with me on Father Christmas's sleigh. I'm very happy because my best friend, Holly the reindeer, has been chosen to fly the sleigh this year. Holly, Eugene, Bells and I love to play Hide and Seek in Lapland. Bells is the best at hiding because he is white and made of snow! Sometimes his hat gives him away though! You can meet all my friends on the next page. First, I have to share something with you, but you have to keep it a secret. Do you promise? Good.

I want you to join us on our journey around the world! You can come with us to Canada, France, Brazil, Britain and beyond! There is one catch, though: you have to play Hide and Seek with us. It won't be easy, but it will be a lot of fun. In each country, you will have to find Father Christmas, Eugene, Holly, Jingle (me) and Bells. I've decided to make it evener harder for you. I have hidden 10 other things you have to find before you can fly to the next country, and I've also hidden a present in there too, as a reward for all your hard work.

Good luck!

Love Jingle

P.S. If you are stuck, the answers can be found in the back of the book.

Merry Christmas Friends!

Ho ho ho.

I hope you have been on your best behaviour! Jingle tells me that you are going to be coming with us on our adventures around the world! I'm very excited you will be joining in the fun during my most favourite time of year. I have had millions of letters delivered to my sorting office in Lapland, and we have been very busy trying to get everything organised. I'm very lucky because Mrs Christmas has been feeding me mince pies and Christmas pudding to keep me going! We're almost ready to begin the journey, so buckle up, have your wits about you and prepare to have the time of your life!

Father Christmas's Helpers

Find out more about Father Christmas's friends and discover what they look like. It will help you find them quicker!

Holly

Holly is very lucky this year because Father Christmas has made her Chief Reindeer. This means she has the very important job of guiding all the other reindeers around the world. This is the first time Holly has been allowed to lead the other reindeers and she is very excited. During the day Holly sleeps in the reindeer barn with Father Christmas's other reindeers, but at night she and her friends practice their flying. Holly is excited to be taking you on your first Christmas adventure around the world!

LIKES: Flying
DISLIKES: Having a cold (in case people mistake her for Rudolph)
FAVOURITE SONG: 'Have Yourself a Merry Little Christmas'
FAVOURITE FOOD: Mince Pies

Jingle

Jingle is Father Christmas's number one Elf. He has been working for Father Christmas for many, many years (that's why his beard is so grey). All year round he helps Father Christmas sort out the mail, keep a close eye on the girls and boys around the world and, towards the end of the year, instructs the younger elves on how to make the best Christmas presents, before loading them all onto the sleigh.

LIKES: Making toys
DISLIKES: Hitting his thumb with his hammer
FAVOURITE SONG: 'Jingle Bells' (because it has his name in it)
FAVOURITE FOOD: Turkey

Bells

Bells lives outside Father Christmas's workshop. He loves the snow and he spends all day building snowballs next to the forest. He is very cheeky because he likes to hide behind the trees and then throw the snowballs he has made at Jingle and the other elves. But Jingle always manages to get his own back on Bells. Sometimes, Jingle throws snowballs at Bells' hat and knocks it off his head! Jingle and Bells play other tricks on each other and they love to play Hide and Seek together.

LIKES: Making snow balls
DISLIKES: The sun (he's scared he might melt)
FAVOURITE SONG: 'Let it Snow! Let it Snow! Let it Snow!'
FAVOURITE FOOD: Carrots

Eugene

Eugene is the coolest penguin in Lapland. When he isn't fishing, Eugene can be found skiing on the slopes and hanging out with Husky dogs. In December, Eugene helps Father Christmas in his workshop testing out all the toys to make sure they work. He also helps Mrs Christmas stamp all the letters Father Christmas has written to all the girls and boys. Eugene is really pleased to meet you and he knows by the end of the journey you will be best of friends!

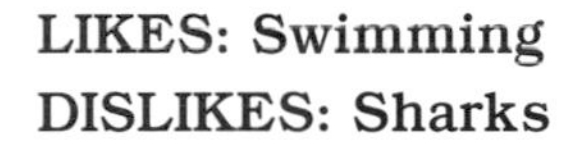

LIKES: Swimming
DISLIKES: Sharks
FAVOURITE SONG: 'Rockin' Around the Christmas Tree'
FAVOURITE FOOD: Squid

Present

Father Christmas and his helpers make hundreds and hundreds of presents. In December they are their most busy, but they wouldn't change places with anyone else because they love making presents for all the good girls and boys. You're very lucky because Father Christmas has made you this special present to find in each country as a reward for all your help!

Lapland
With more presents than ever to deliver, the elves are wrapping as fast as they can. They're nearly ready for the big day, but where is Father Christmas? Will you be able to find him and his helpers in time to deliver all the presents?
Fun fact: Father Christmas's main post office is located on the Arctic Circle line in Finnish Lapland.
12 candy canes
A pint of milk
A robot
An elf in a tutu
A bright blue Christmas stocking
A bunch of carrots
A rag doll
An oversized, striped red and blue sock
The Finnish flag
An elf reading a book
P
C
B
D
EC
24
PLAN A.
24 DEC
CHECK LIST
NICE
NICE
NAUGHTY

NICE
SWEE TS

Norway
Uh-oh, it looks as though the Norwegians have left it until the last minute to buy their Christmas tree, and now Father Christmas and friends have been caught up in all the commotion. Can you find them so they can get back on their sleigh?
Fun fact: Christmas trees became common in Norway around 1900 – that's over 100 years ago.
A polar bear
A red and white striped scarf
A snowboard
Ice cream
Mistletoe
A compass
An Arctic fox
A candle
The Norwegian flag
An Eskimo

S.C.

Bratwurs
Confectionery
S.C.

Germany

Father Christmas and his friends have landed in Germany and it's good timing, too! The market is in full swing and everyone is getting in the festive spirit, eating Pretzels and shopping for gifts. But it's so busy that Father Christmas has managed to get lost with his friends. Can you see him in the crowds?

Fun fact: The custom of having Christmas trees is originally from Germany.

- ☐ A pink and yellow lolly
- ☐ A boy in green lederhosen
- ☐ The German flag
- ☐ A gnome
- ☐ 4 people eating Pretzels
- ☐ A snow globe
- ☐ A gingerbread man
- ☐ Candyfloss
- ☐ A man selling popcorn
- ☐ A lady with an orange bag

Great Britain
Father Christmas has landed in Britain after a very short ride from Germany! It's very busy in Trafalgar Square, London. People have been out shopping for decorations and presents, and now they are gathering in the Square to hear Christmas carols. It looks like Father Christmas has arrived just in time to join in the fun!
Fun fact: The Trafalgar Square Christmas tree is donated to the people of London by the city of Oslo each year and has been a tradition since 1947.
A man holding an umbrella
A bulldog
A teapot
A candy cane
The Queen
A daffodil
A briefcase
The English flag
An acorn
A black and white cat

S.C.
TOUR
NEWS

The SHACK
BBQ
S.C

Australia

Father Christmas has landed his sleigh in Australia and it's boiling hot! The lucky Australians get to celebrate Christmas in the sunshine rather than snow! Even though it's Christmas everyone is on the beach! It looks as though Father Christmas is enjoying the sunshine a bit too much! Can you see him sunbathing?

Fun fact: During the Christmas period, Australians often decorate their homes with ferns, palm leaves and evergreens, along with colourful flowers.

- ☐ A lilo
- ☐ A green BBQ
- ☐ A red baseball cap
- ☐ A starfish
- ☐ A volleyball
- ☐ Red sunglasses
- ☐ A man in orange swimming shorts
- ☐ A lady in polka-dot bikini
- ☐ The Australian flag
- ☐ A man in a furry coat

S.C.

China
After a quick flight over Singapore, Father Christmas has landed on the Great Wall of China! There are hundreds of people celebrating on the Wall, and it's wonderfully colourful. Father Christmas has been enjoying himself too much. Help find him so we can fly to the United States on time, otherwise we may not be able to deliver the presents!
Fun fact: Contrary to common belief, the Great Wall of China cannot be seen from the moon.
A rabbit
A man with a beard and moustache
10 people eating with chopsticks
A sword
A dragon
A lady with pink hair
Pink and blue striped firework
The Chinese flag
A panda
A violin

THE CONCOURSE
ROCKEFELLER CENTER
NYC
S.C.

United States of America

Father Christmas loves visiting New York in the States. He loves flying over all the tall skyscrapers and Central Park late at night. It's always busy in NYC, the place that never sleeps, and Father Christmas is struggling to deliver the presents! Help find him so he can get on his way!

Fun fact: The Christmas tree outside the Rockefeller Centre is normally erected in late November and has been a tradition since 1933.

- ☐ A man with ski goggles on
- ☐ A women in red skate boots
- ☐ A girl holding a balloon
- ☐ The Statue of Liberty
- ☐ An apple
- ☐ The US flag
- ☐ An alien
- ☐ A hot dog
- ☐ Someone with a broken arm
- ☐ An American footballer

House
Here is a sneak peek of Father Christmas delivering his presents inside a lucky person's house! The only problem is he has arrived too early and everyone is still up celebrating! Father Christmas has to pretend he is in fancy dress so they don't find out it's really him.
Puppy with a bow around its neck
A holly wreath
A Christmas pudding
A Christmas cracker
Wooden logs
Rocking horse
The North star
A tin soldier
A ginger cat
Mince pies

BORG

Canada

Eugene, Bells, Holly and Jingle are happy to be in Canada because it's snowing and it reminds them of home! They were very excited to join in the fun on the ski slopes but now they are lost! Father Christmas went to find them and now he is lost, too. Can you find them?

Fun fact: The first Christmas stamp was released in Canada in 1898.

- [ ] The Canadian flag
- [ ] A red and white scarf
- [ ] Bobsleigh
- [ ] An icicle
- [ ] Someone with a broken leg
- [ ] A carrot
- [ ] A fur hat
- [ ] Someone looking at a map
- [ ] An owl
- [ ] Rainbow coloured goggles

MAP
S.C.

TOUR

Poland

After a wonderful stop in Canada, Father Christmas is in Poland. He loves the beautiful castle in Kraków. People have gathered outside to sing songs and celebrate Christmas before they go home to cook lots of yummy food!

Fun fact: Polish people consider spiders to be symbols of goodness and prosperity at Christmas.

- ☐ The Polish flag
- ☐ A mouse
- ☐ A scarecrow
- ☐ A knight's helmet
- ☐ A princess
- ☐ A girl dancing
- ☐ A man reading the newspaper
- ☐ A clipboard
- ☐ A beer bottle
- ☐ A chicken

Brazil
Father Christmas loves to dance, so it's a good job the Brazilians like to Samba dance. He was excited to join in the celebrations on the streets, but now he has got lost in the crowd. Can you find him?
Fun fact: In Brazil Christmas is one of the most important festive days, or 'dia de festas'.
Sun cream
Flip-flops
A red balloon
A pink feather boa
A parrot
The Brazilian flag
A cocktail
A snake
A man on his phone
A football
S.C.

South Africa
The sun is out, there are beautiful flowers in full bloom and even the animals are out celebrating Christmas. Eugene and Holly are excited to meet other animals, even lions! Father Christmas has stepped off his sleigh and swapped it for a safari jeep to deliver the presents. Have you found him yet?
Fun fact: South Africa is in the southern hemisphere, so Christmas comes in the summer.
A meerkat
The South African flag
A lion
A Zulu shield
A beetle
A flamingo
A grey suitcase
Binoculars
A handheld fan
A picnic hamper

SAFARI MAP.

Italy
After enjoying the South African sun, Father Christmas has pulled up his sleigh in Italy. At the moment, he is enjoying some sightseeing in Pisa. Can you find him and his friends before he gets lost?
Fun fact: Homemade fettuccine and ravioli are often served on Christmas day in Italy.
A pizza slice
Racing car
A pigeon
A chef
An ice cream
A dog in a handbag
The Italian flag
An opera singer
Orange sunglasses
Blue earmuffs
S.C.

France

Father Christmas has nearly finished delivering his presents, although there are still a few other countries he has to visit. Father Christmas loves France, especially Paris. The Eiffel Tower always looks beautiful at night when he flies over it on his sleigh.

Fun fact: In France Christmas is called '*Noël*'.

- [ ] An artist
- [ ] A ballerina
- [ ] A baguette
- [ ] The French flag
- [ ] A frog
- [ ] A saxophone
- [ ] Two mime artists
- [ ] A robin
- [ ] A street light
- [ ] A croissant

RUE
LA RUE
MENU
MENU
S.C.
PARIS MAP

Ho, Ho, Ho

It's time for Father Christmas to head home, but not before picking out a tree for his house. Uh-oh, it looks like lots of helpers have joined him – and they are all dressed like Father Christmas! Can you find them all?

☐ Add them all up and put your answer here.

GUIDE

Answers

Did you spot Father Christmas's helper? Mrs Christmas jumped on the sleigh and has been hiding too. Go back through the illustrations and look for her! If you can't find her, she is circled in the answers below.

Lapland

Norway

Bratwurst.
Confectionery
Bar.
DRINKS
TEA
COFFEE
MILK
DRINKS
TEA
COFFEE
MILK
CHOCO
MEAD
Germany

TOUR
NEWS
Great Britain

The SHACK
BBQ
Australia

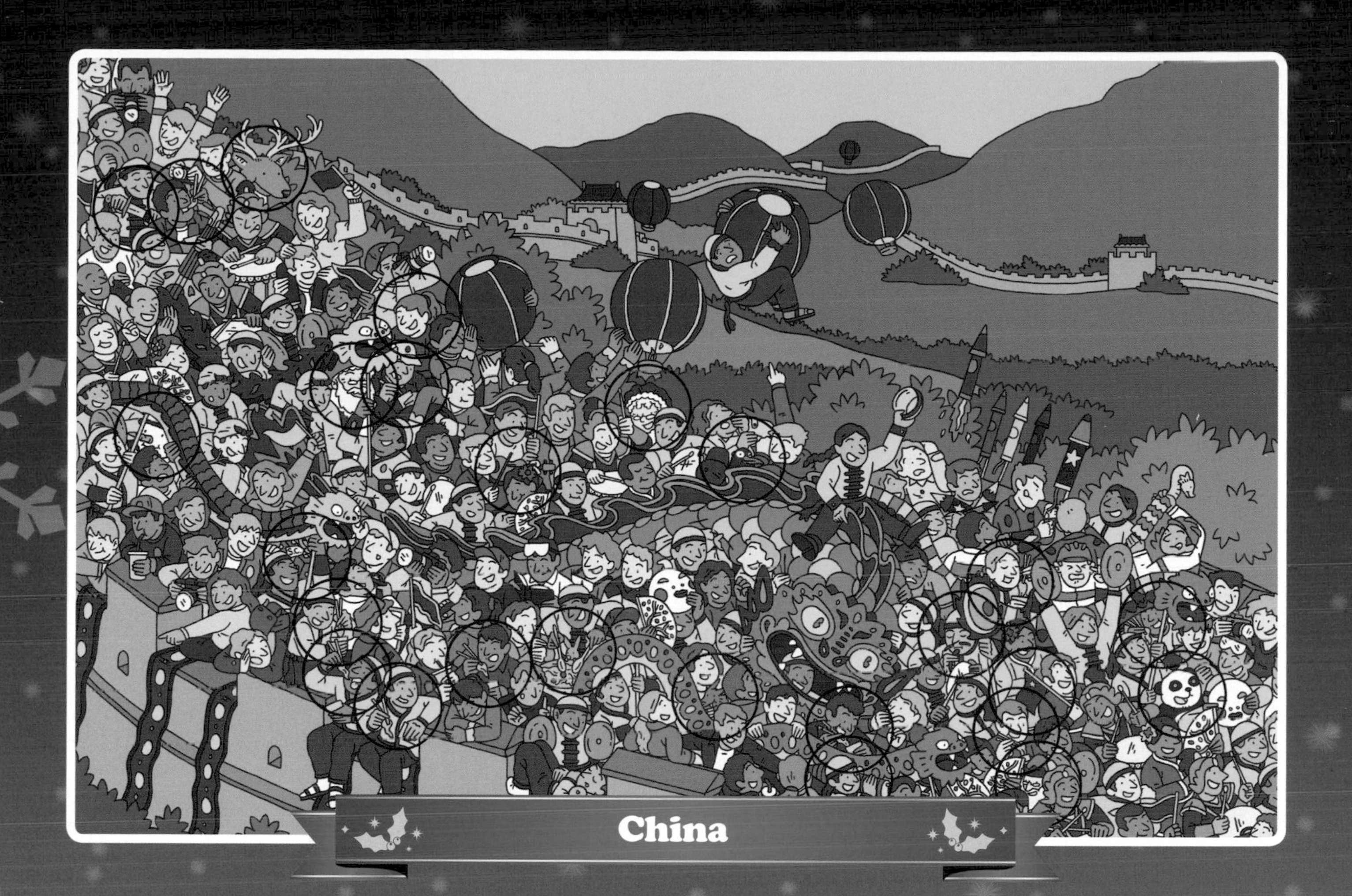

China

United States of America

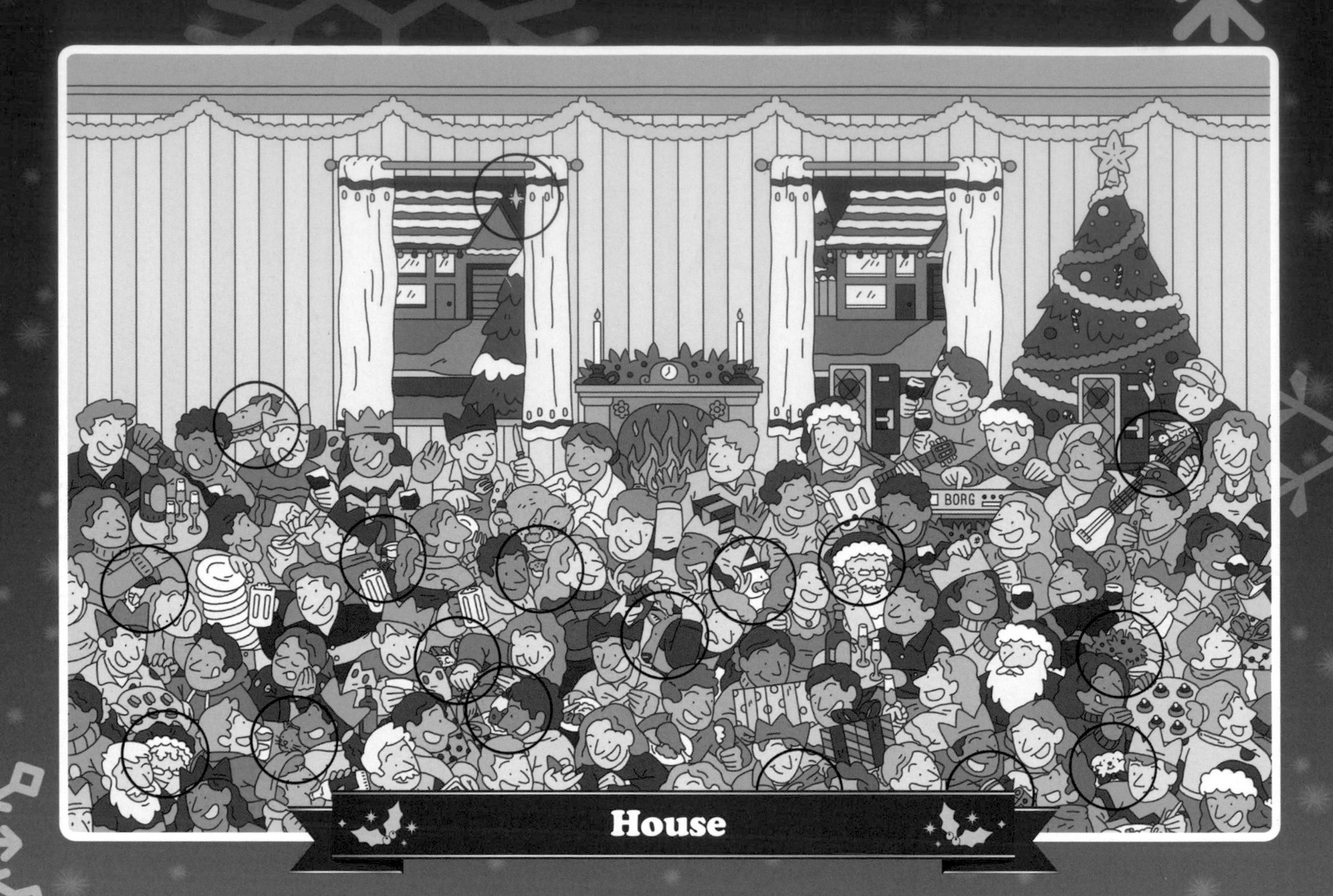

House

Canada

Poland

Brazil

South Africa

Italy

France

Ho, Ho, Ho

S.C.